The Forgotten Ones

The Lives of Senior Shelter Dogs
As Told by Onyx

REBECCA SAPP

Illustrated by Sierra Mon Ann Vidal

To order additional copies of this book, contact:
Xlibris
1-888-795-4274
www.Xlibris.com
Orders@Xlibris.com

ISBN: Softcover   978-1-7960-8302-6
        Hardcover   978-1-7960-9285-1
        EBook   978-1-7960-8301-9

Print information available on the last page

Rev. date: 01/15/2020

This author gives special thanks and appreciation to Dogwood Animal Shelter for their dedication to the many dogs and cats residing here. They truly love the animals and care for them without fail. The devotion to them is heartfelt and it is an honor to help bring awareness to the need for increased senior shelter animal adoption.

Introduction
Facts on Senior Dogs

Many of our senior dogs are forgotten about in our communities. While pet adoption has risen, a problem still exists for our senior dogs. Many people may be unaware that our senior animals in shelters are growing in numbers. They are being looked over, because they are not quite the perfect dog; older in age or have special needs or physical limitations.

Dogs will remember the smallest act of kindness. These animals are capable of loyalty, protection, companionship, and love. Every dog, no matter how old or young deserves to experience the feeling of love in their lifetime.

So, please, when you are walking down those corridors and have already made that first decision to adopt, take your time. Senior animals make wonderful companions. Please consider giving a senior dog a chance to be part of your family.

It's a very dark, stormy night and I'm a young puppy who has wandered away from home. My home was an old crate under a bridge with my brothers and sisters. Since my Mother had gone looking for food for us I decided to start chasing rabbits for fun. I was chasing a rabbit and it disappeared and then realized nothing looked familiar and I was near the highway.

From behind the bushes and tall grass cars are honking and zooming by me and I'm afraid. It is raining harder and harder and lightning and thunder are all around. In the distance I see a light and to me that meant help. I ran as fast as my long skinny legs could go across the highway dodging cars and trucks and then I saw a cottage right in front of me.

I could make out an outline of a little white cottage with a porch. Suddenly feeling a tiny bit brave, I climbed onto the porch. I made the biggest bark I could do, Woof, Woof and scratched at the door.

Suddenly the door flew open and to my surprise a little old woman with white hair scooped me up and ran back inside, slamming the door shut.

The woman must have known that I was afraid because she held me close even though I was a wet, muddy mess. "I won't hurt you," she said.

Before I knew what was happening, she was bathing me; next warming me in a soft blanket. She began rocked me in front of the fireplace till I was dry.

"You sure are a skinny girl," she laughed.

She had no dog food, so she shared her meal with me. I'd never had meatloaf and potatoes and I ate so fast, my tail wagging the entire time. After finishing eating; my tummy full, I was content and getting sleepy. The lady let me sit in her lap while she rocked in her chair.

"I don't know what I should call you. Do you mind the name Onyx? It's a beautiful black gem, and your fur is black."

My tail wagged, and that's how I got my name. She was my first friend and I'm very proud of how I was named. She let me sleep with her that night so I wouldn't be afraid. She was so kind.

The next morning was another delicious meal while she talked softly and brushed my fur. She talked to me like I understood exactly what she was saying. I did know she was kind and good to me. She told me she couldn't keep me, because she was going to go to live with her daughter. She knew a place not far away that helped dogs and cats in need.

She could take me without any problem, so I needed to trust her.

Later that morning the lady put me in the front seat of her old pickup and drove the short distance to Dogwood Animal Shelter.

She could tell I felt unsure and said, "It's ok Onyx. These people will help find you a family, and until that time they will care for you." She patted my head and I wished I could stay with her.

We got out of the truck and walked up to the building. The lady had me wrapped in a blanket since it was chilly outside. As we walked through the entrance doors, I looked on both sides of the building. On one side were cats playing in two rooms; climbing, batting balls, and napping in sunny windows.

On the other side of the room were small dogs, a few puppies and a couple of children in the floor playing ball and tug of war with a rope. One of the children that caught my attention had three dogs in her lap and was laughing and playing in the floor with dogs climbing all over her. The workers were calling her Sophia. She seemed a lot of fun and had pretty long blonde hair. She was laughing while the dogs were barking.

At the big desk a friendly lady took me from my nice white-haired lady.

"Thank you for bringing her in, we'll take good care of her."

My lady had tears in her eyes as she turned to leave.

"Thank you, her name is Onyx." And then she was gone. I was the newest resident of Dogwood Animal Shelter. My new adventure has begun.

The new lady put me over her shoulder while juggling a pile of paperwork at the same time. I looked around nervously. The pups were still playing in the hallway with Sophia and she softly spoke to me as we walked past her, "Hey, let's play someday, it'll be fun," I wagged my tail at her. That sounded great!

We walked down the hall and I saw a small shaggy brown dog in an open room. I yipped at him happily. A sign on the door read Fred. He just growled back as if to say, "I don't know you well enough to talk to you yet", so we walked on. A sweet little old black pug yapped at me.

"My name is Maggie, What's yours?"

I excitedly replied, "I'm Onyx."

I couldn't believe I might already have friends. I started to think things might be ok here.

After the checkup with the vet we were going down the corridor near where I would sleep, and I met one of my neighbors named Levi. Levi was a funny mix of a dog, medium build, brownish in color. The thing that stuck in my mind about Levi was that he still has such a happy face; even after telling me he had been here quite a long time. His dream was to have his own boy to play tug of war with and to play frisbee every day. It made me feel sad that such a simple wish could not come true for this nice dog.

"You have to keep the hope, Levi,"

"I will, Onyx. I'm glad you're my neighbor. I won't give up!"

The lady showed me to my new kennel. It wasn't the white-haired lady's house and it was certainly wasn't my Mother's home under the bridge. I was sad missing my Mother and family, but I slowly settled into the shelter routine.

There are many different people working here. There are staff members and many volunteers' that come in regularly, but all are kind.

As time went on, I met more of the dogs at the shelter. The ones I found had been there the longest were the older dogs and dogs with special needs. This concerned me because these dogs were great dogs. I believe all of them should be given a chance to show love to a family. How can this be done? There had to be a way to help these dogs.

One of my neighbors, Scooter, seemed particularly sad because he had not been adopted. He didn't want to come out and play anymore. He so much missed having a person to love that his spirit was broken. He had a man a long time ago. He knew that feeling of being loved and missed it. I wanted so much to help him.

Ginger is another amazing dog here at the shelter. She is nine years old and has been here almost nine years. She is healthy, and sweet spirited. She loves taking long walks, playing fetch, and when I talk to Ginger her only wish is to know what it feels like to have a real home.

"I really admire her strength. I want her to know what love is like."

Amber is a pretty white whippet mix that's been here awhile also, and she's a real sweetheart. I thought she was going to get adopted the other day. She got so excited. A family was going to adopt her, and a funny little dog named Lucky also, but it did not happen. Amber was so disappointed. She loves children. Lucky got adopted a few days later, but without his friend Amber.

A special thing did happen for me. One day my worker came to get me from my kennel. I had been approved for a program called Puppies on Parole. This was a program where certain dogs were sent to a prison to work with approved inmates one on one for eight weeks. The dogs would learn obedience training and at the end of the training they would be proficient in dog obedience and have an award and a certificate for their achievement. I was so proud but wished I had someone to share it with. Now that I graduated the program it was now time for me to be sent back to Dogwood Animal Shelter. It was good to be back home.

I was now over two years old and I sometimes wonder if I would ever have a fur -ever home? I try to stay positive and focus on the good in my life. I tell all my friends, *"Don't give up hope"*!

Some things had changed at the shelter while I was gone. I now see big yellow school buses often drive up to our building filled with lots of children. The children are given tours of our shelter and they get to see all the dogs and cats. We enjoy the children and they always seem happy to see us.

Spice is an older dog who has also been here for years and she especially looks forward to the children because she rarely gets any visits other than from them. People don't want the dogs that are flawed or have some age on them. They should know that dogs have so much love to give. I wish I could make Spice's life better.

One morning I hadn't been awake long when a loud buzzer went off. I laughed to myself. That could only mean Mikey was on the run again. Mikey is a very good dog and like many of the senior dogs that do not get many visitors; he gets bored and has learned to play a game of catch me if you can with the finish line being the front door. Mikey went one way and the workers ran in the other direction. He has such a great sense of humor.

"You see, he has a great respect for doors. He sees a door so he will sit in front of it until someone opens it."

One worker patted Mikey on the head, "Ok boy, your run is over, I guess I needed one also" laughing, and back they went.

A few weeks later I saw something rather wondrous happen that I will always remember. It was a midday afternoon and I was taking a lazy nap in my kennel when the big metal door opened. We all knew the sound and we immediately sat up trying to look and act our best. This could mean someone was here looking for a dog to adopt. I could hear footsteps coming down my corridor. They were soft steps and were coming closer. I tried to stand straight at attention but felt myself shaking. I saw a woman coming closer, then going past me. My heart fell. Again, I was passed over. Why? I didn't know. But I collected myself and watched. The woman stopped a few kennels down at my friend Riley's kennel. He was a little corgi mix and had been here a long time. I saw her reading his card. I hoped in reading his past it wouldn't make her afraid and move on. She stopped reading and bent down. She had on old clothes, very worn. Her hair was long and wind-blown, greyish in color. She had a weathered, sad look to her face. She put her hand on the fence. He immediately licked her hand. She went in the kennel, stooped and petted his head. Suddenly he leaped up in her arms. Tears started pouring down her face and his stubby tail wagged. I quietly barked my support. He was my friend.

"Riley, you did it. Congratulations, buddy. You always said you were going to get chosen by a human, and well you kept the hope and you did it."

I watched the pair walk off together. He had waited so long, but it had happened. I was so happy for them. He finally had his fur ever home.

Months passed and I was just coming in from my morning jog around the grounds with one of the volunteers when I heard my name called in the kennel room. Being taken to the playroom by my worker was a treat in itself. That didn't happen every day for us older dogs.

When I was being taken off my leash, I saw one of my favorite volunteers, Sophia.

We had briefly played here and there but I had never had her for my very own playmate. She was finishing up a game of tug of war with Levi and I think he was winning. To his surprise she started tickling his ears and she won! Little pup Everest followed Sophia around. Pretty, shy Willow always let her pet her dark, smooth head, and Tex, well, he was just proud to be seen with her. Tex was a beautiful dog who would make such a great companion to somebody. He is a long timer here also. So, as Sophia is saying goodbye to all her other friends for the day, I am patiently waiting for my time with her. Time well worth waiting for.

Sophia bent down on one knee to talk to me.

"Onyx, I'm Sophia. I bet we are going to be good friends and I come here to play all the time and I'd like to play with you."

She looked right into my eyes and I liked that. It's as if we understood each other. She sat down and I crawled into her lap. We did that for a few minutes with her just gently petting my head and my ears. It felt really good. I felt at ease with her.

"Do you want to run?" I looked up at her.

No one ever asks that. I barked happily and started running all over the room with her at my side. What a wonderful day. We ran until we both fell in a big heap in the middle of the playroom floor.

"I'm so glad we got to know each other. It's nice having a new friend. If you'd like, I'll keep coming back to play with you? I promise you.!"

We both got up and walked to the door together standing close. Sophia put her hand on my head then bent down and kissed me on the nose and whispered, "Bye for now, I'll be back, I love you." It sure is hard leaving a new friend.

As I sprinted to my kennel with my head held high and tail wagging, I am very happy. I have made a special friend and yes, I have hope for my future at Dogwood Animal Shelter. I have friends and I am a good dog.

The next couple of days were busy for me. More new dogs have come to the shelter. A few more have been adopted; None being senior dogs. That makes me sad. We all want to feel what it is to be loved. I was beginning to wonder if we all would get that chance. I do my best to keep our spirits up.

It is playtime for me and that means that my friend Sophia just might be in that playroom. As I'm rounding the corner on my leash, I see my friend Konner. A pretty red dog who was very smart. He was so smart he could paint.

"Hey Onyx, my foster mom is buying me longer paint brushes so I can paint better, isn't that great? That's sure to help me get a home."

I answered back, "Well, if you do, remember your friends, you are smart and beautiful. You will find a home."

Sophia kept her promise and has come back to play again. Today was a quieter day so we played outside. When we tired, we sat on the bench for a rest and watched the leaves blow. I reached up to kiss her and she laughed and in return hugged me tight. We have a special relationship.

"Onyx, I know our time together is special, but you deserve your own home and family. I'm promising you that I'm going to try to find people to help you and all your animal friends find homes. Until you do find your fur ever family I'll keep coming back. Friends fur ever!"

THE END

Printed in the United States
By Bookmasters